ICE AGE

THE MOVIE NOVEL

ADAPTATION BY J.E. BRIGHT

HarperEntertainment
An Imprint of HarperCollins*Publishers*

HarperCollins books are available at special quantity discounts for bulk purchases for sales promotions, premiums, or fund-raising. For information please call or write: Special Markets Department, HarperCollins Publishers Inc., 10 East 53rd Street, New York, NY 10022.

HarperCollins®, 📖®, and HarperEntertainment™ are trademarks of HarperCollins Publishers Inc.

ISBN 0-06-093815-3

First printing: February 2002

Visit HarperEntertainment on the World Wide Web at www.harpercollins.com

10 9 8 7 6 5 4 3 2 1

CONTENTS

CHAPTER ONE

Freezing wind swept across a barren plain of ice.

A little squirrel-like critter called a scrat scurried over the wasteland. The scrat carried a big acorn in his mouth.

He stopped and tried to jam his acorn into the ice, hoping to store his winter harvest. No matter how hard the scrat pushed, the acorn wouldn't break through the frozen crust. He hopped on it, forcing it down with all his weight.

With a frighteningly loud groan, a zigzagging crack broke the ice near the acorn. The scrat watched with wide, frightened eyes as the crack lengthened, unzipping across the icy plain, snapping a mountainous glacier in half. One piece of the glacier slammed into another, setting off a domino effect. Vast sections of ice tumbled onto the white field.

The scrat screamed. The falling mountains of ice crashed all around him, squashing the landscape, flattening trees. Grabbing his acorn, the tiny animal skittered across the plain. A tunnel of ice formed around him, narrowing suddenly, trapping him. He pushed forward, trying to force his way out. After a moment, the pressure of the moving ice behind him shot the scrat out of the tiny tunnel. He launched into the bright blue sky.

As he soared through the air, he spotted his acorn sailing beside him. He grabbed it and smiled.

Then the scrat noticed how high above the ground he was. He screamed again, dropping his acorn and plunging toward the plain below.

With a loud thud, the scrat hit the ground. After a few moments, he sat up, dazed. His acorn whacked him on the head, knocking him down again. He sat up once more before he was squashed again, this time by a giant foot.

When the foot lifted, the scrat peered around groggily. Through swirling dust, he could see a vast convoy of enormous animals heading south through a gigantic broken pass in the ice wall. Another heavy foot squished the scrat, and he stuck to the hoof like a chewed-up piece of gum. The scrat whimpered as he was dragged away from his acorn.

Near the front of the migration line, two freaky mammals waddled south. One craned his head toward his companion. "But how do we *know* it's an Ice Age?" he asked.

"Because of all the *ice*!" the other freaky mammal yelled.

The ground began to shake with thunderous footsteps. A gigantic, majestic creature lumbered through the crowd like an eighteen-wheel truck driving the wrong way through traffic. The giant animal had thick, matted orange-brown fur and sweeping, curved tusks. His name was Manfred.

"Spread out! Comin' through," the mammoth announced.

Little animals scurried out of Manfred's path. "Where're you goin'?" one animal called out.

"What are you doing?" another one shouted. "We're migrating here!"

A family of stocky beasts with stubby little trunks watched the woolly mammoth fight his way against traffic.

"Hey!" the father shouted to Manfred. "Do the world a favor and move your issues off the road!"

Manfred whipped out his trunk and grabbed the

creature around the neck, pulling him close. "If my trunk was that small," he growled, "I wouldn't draw attention to myself, pal."

The animal trembled. "Give me a break," he muttered. "We've been waddling all day."

Manfred glanced up and saw the rest of the family watching with worried eyes. The burly mammoth sighed and put the father down on the ground. "Ah, go ahead, follow the crowd," he said. Manfred pushed past the family and continued north through the throng of animals. "It'll be quieter when you're gone."

The mother rushed to her mate. "Don't listen to him, dear," she cooed. "I love your trunk just the way it is."

"C'mon," the father said gruffly as he began to waddle south again. "If he wants to freeze to death, let him."

Near the northern point of the river valley, the migrating animals filed past a tree. A chubby, sloppy sloth named Sid was spread out on a branch, fast asleep and snoring loudly. As the migration thundered by, the branch the sloth was on bounced up and down. With each thud, he slipped farther and farther off the branch, finally ending upside down, hanging by his claws and swinging wildly. He woke up, surprised, and peered around.

"Zak!" he called, checking the branch next to his. "Marshall?" He climbed down to the ground. "Uncle Fungus?" There wasn't a single other sloth in sight.

"I don't believe it. They left without me." Sid threw his arms wide and howled at the sky. "Isn't there anyone who cares about Sid?" He buried his face in his hands and sobbed.

"Sidney?" a female voice squealed. "Sidney!"

Sid froze. "Anyone but her," he muttered. A young female sloth waddled toward him with her arms outstretched. Her name was Sylvia, and Sid was far from thrilled to see her. He hurried behind the tree to hide. Sylvia followed him.

"Sidney, I can't believe it," she burbled. "You waited for me! Now we can migrate together."

"No, no. I just happen to not be migrating this year, that's all." He eyed a nearby cave and got an idea. "I've decided to hibernate. I mean, how hard could it be? Gorge yourself on food and sleep it off for three months? I've been training my whole life for that." He disappeared into the cave.

Sylvia followed him in and came back out carrying Sid over her shoulder. "Nice try, Sidney, but sloths don't hibernate."

"But I think I can do it! My metabolism is really slow!"

"You wanna know why you showed up this morning, Sidney? Because deep down you know I'm the sloth for you."

Sid spotted a pack of armored glyptodons bustling toward Sylvia from behind her. He smirked, struck with an idea. "You know, you're right," he said. "I can't fight destiny anymore." Making sure Sylvia couldn't see the glyptodons, he steered her around until she stood directly in their path. He smiled. "Let me get a look at you," he said warmly.

Sylvia's face glowed. "Oh, *Sidney*." At that moment, the squat glyptodons bumped into Sylvia's legs. She tumbled on top of them. The glyptodons swept past Sid, carrying Sylvia down the migratory route. Sylvia screamed in dismay.

Sid started jogging in place, pretending he was running to rescue her. "Where are you going?" he cried in fake alarm. "Reach for me!"

"Sidney!" Sylvia screeched as the glyptodons hauled her away.

"Don't worry, honey bunny!" Sid yelled. "We'll find each other!"

The glyptodons carried Sylvia around a corner. Once she disappeared from sight, Sid stopped pretending to jog.

"Whew," he said, sighing in relief. "That was close."

CHAPTER TWO

As Sid dawdled back toward the cave, something mushy squished under his paw. "Ohhh, sick!" Sid whined. He'd stepped in a steaming pile of glyptodon poop.

Sid glared at the glyptodon waddling away. "Hey, *widebody*!" he screamed. "Curb it next time!"

Stomping on the ground, Sid tried to shake the dung from his paws. But the stuff was clingy, so he slid his paw along the grass. "Yuck."

Nearby, two muscular rhinoceroses stood beside a large, elegant salad of crisp leaves that they'd collected. "I can't believe it," the rhino named Carl said happily. "Fresh wild greens." He turned to the other rhino and smiled. "Frank, where did you ever find—"

"Go ahead," Frank interrupted, pleased. "Dig in."

Then Carl noticed a little yellow flower garnishing the salad. "A dandelion!" Carl gasped. "I thought the frost wiped them all out."

"All but one," Frank replied.

Carl opened his mouth to take a bite. Before he had a chance, Sid hopped onto the bed of tasty leaves, still stomping and scraping his paw to get it clean. "Aw, yuck!" the sloth exclaimed.

Completely oblivious to the disgusting damage he was doing to the rhinoceroses' lunch, Sid grabbed onto Frank's horn so that he could clean his paw more easily. "This has definitely not been my day," he told Frank. "You know what I'm saying, buddy?" Sid finished tidying up his paws. "Gosh, what a mess." He patted Frank's head as if the rhino was a puppy. "Hey, did you know rhinos have really tiny brains? It's a fact, no offense." Sid waved his hand dismissively. "Ah, you probably don't even know what I'm talking about."

Then Sid spotted the dandelion. "Oh, yummo!" he cheered, snatching it. "Must be the last one of the season." He popped the flower into his mouth.

Carl glared at Sid so furiously that steam should have been coming out of his ears.

"Mmm," Sid murmured as he chewed. It was a particularly delicious dandelion. "Mmm!"

"*Carl,*" Frank growled, boiling with fury.

Finally, Sid noticed what he'd done to the rhinoceroses' food. He jumped off the ruined salad. "Oh, my mistake, fellas!" Hurrying to get away, Sid tripped over a fallen log and tumbled onto his face.

He quickly pulled himself up again. "Let me make it up to you," he told the infuriated rhinos. Sid spied a bunch of large seedpods on the ground and picked one up. "What's this?" he asked. "A pinecone! Oh my goodness, they're my favorite!" He stuffed the pinecone in his mouth and chewed. His chomping made a terrible sound like crunching broken glass.

"Mmm," Sid lied. "Delicious. That's—" He swallowed painfully. "Good eating. But don't let me hog them all up. Here!" Sid picked up more pinecones and stuffed them into Carl's mouth. "Have some."

Carl's eyes blazed as Sid forced the rhino's jaw up and down in a chewing motion.

"Mmm," Sid said weakly as the pinecones crunched. "Tasty?"

Carl growled.

Sid flashed him a big, fake smile. "*Bon appétit!*" he exclaimed, and then he sped away as fast as his short, thick legs would carry him.

"Now?" Frank asked.

"Now," Carl replied.

The rhinoceroses lowered their horns and charged.

When Sid glanced back and saw the rhinos thundering toward him, he let out a scream and zipped around the corner of the hillside.

He slammed into a huge, hairy hind leg.

"Oof!" Sid cried.

"Hey!" a booming voice protested.

Sid glanced up at the enormous mammoth he'd bumped into. It was Manfred. Sid took one look at the powerful mammal with his sharp, curving tusks and scrambled behind him to hide. "Just pretend I'm not here!" Sid yelped.

Manfred faced the rhinos rumbling toward him.

The rhinoceroses slowed when they saw the mammoth. "Man," Frank complained. "I wanted to hit him at full speed."

"That's okay, Frank," Carl replied. "We'll have some fun with him."

Sid clamped his arms around Manfred's tree trunk of a back leg. "Don't let them impale me!" he cried. "Please! I want to live!"

Manfred shook Sid loose. "Get off me," he grumbled.

The second Sid hit the ground, he popped up and desperately hid behind Manfred again.

"C'mon," Carl called to Sid. "You're making a scene."

"We'll just take our furry piñata and go," Frank told the mammoth, "if you don't mind."

Manfred peered down at Sid. "If it's not them today," he said to the sloth, "it'll just be someone else tomorrow."

"I'd rather it not be today," Sid replied. "Okay?"

"We'll break your neck so you don't feel a thing," Carl suggested. "How's that?"

Manfred narrowed his eyes suspiciously. "Wait a minute," he said. "I thought rhinos were vegetarians."

"An excellent point!" Sid added.

"Shut up," the mammoth hissed.

Carl shrugged. "Who says we're gonna eat him after we kill him?"

"You know," Manfred said with a growl, "I don't like animals who kill for pleasure."

"Save it for a mammal who cares," Carl replied.

Sid peered around Manfred. "*I'm* a mammal who cares!"

The rhinoceroses stomped closer to Manfred and Sid, intent on attacking the cowering sloth.

"How about this?" Manfred asked. "If either of you make it across the sinkhole in front of you, you get the sloth."

The rhinoceroses had skeptical expressions on

their faces, but they slowed down. They glanced at the moist ground in front of them, which suddenly seemed swampy and ominous.

Sid stuck his head out from behind Manfred's leg. "That's right, you losers!" he shouted. "You take one step and you're dead!" To prove his point, Sid grabbed a heavy rock and tossed it onto the sinkhole.

The rock landed with a *thud*. It didn't sink an inch.

Sheepishly, Sid retreated behind the mammoth's leg. "You were bluffing, huh?"

"Yeah," Manfred confirmed. "That was a bluff."

"Get them!" Carl hollered.

He and Frank lowered their heads and charged. The rhinos slammed into the mammoth, pushing him backward—right toward the edge of a cliff!

Sid threw his slight body against Manfred's leg, helping him push back against the rhino assault. When Sid noticed the steep, rocky slope directly behind him, he screamed a high-pitched wail of terror.

Manfred dug his feet into the ground and shoved the rhinoceroses with his massive shoulder. Carl and Frank flipped onto their backs, their stumpy legs flailing.

"*Woo-hoo!*" Sid cheered, waving his arms like a champion boxer.

The rhinos rolled right-side-up and charged. Their sharp horns glinted with menace.

Sid shrieked. He scrambled to hide behind Manfred.

As Carl rumbled at the mammoth, Manfred whipped out his strong trunk and wrapped it around the rhino's horn. With a grunt, Manfred lifted the whole rhinoceros off the ground. Then he slammed him down—hard.

Carl slumped where he'd been smashed, his eyes rolling crazily. His gaze landed on a tender yellow flower near his snout. "A dandelion," Carl said with a sigh.

Frank focused on impaling Sid. Before the rhino reached the sloth, Manfred scooped Frank up with his curved tusks. Then he hurled the rhino in the air.

Frank fell heavily, flattening Carl's dandelion into pulp.

Sid raised his arms triumphantly again. "We did it!" he shouted. "Yeah!" He hugged Manfred's trunk.

The sudden burst of gratitude caught Manfred off guard. He stumbled backward, and the mammoth and the sloth began to slide down the rocky mountainside. Sid screeched the whole way.

Manfred landed at the bottom with a *thump* that shook the landscape. Sid clung to the mammoth's face, plastered there in fear. When Manfred opened his big eyes, Sid's face was so close that his eyeballs were nearly touching Manfred's.

"You have beautiful eyes," Sid whispered sincerely.

"Get off"—Manfred grunted—"my face." He reared his head, flinging Sid loose. The mammoth lumbered to his feet and walked away.

Sid hopped up and followed. "Whoa!" he called. "We make a great team. What do you say we head south together?"

The mammoth pretended to look thrilled. "Great!" he said enthusiastically. "Yeah! Jump up on my back and relax the whole way!"

"Wow," Sid replied with a smile. "Really?"

"No," Manfred replied. He turned to walk away again—heading due north.

"Wait," the sloth shouted. "Aren't you going south? The change of seasons? Migration instinct? Any of this ringing a bell?"

"Guess not," Manfred called as he marched northward. "Bye."

Sid puffed up his narrow chest, trying to feel brave. "Okay, then," he announced. "Thanks for the help. I can take it from here."

The sloth peered up the cliff he and Manfred had just tumbled down. Carl and Frank were on their feet, glaring at him from the top of the slope.

"Hey, get back up here!" Carl hollered angrily. "And bring us something to kill you with!"

Sid whirled around and raced after Manfred. "Whoa, wait up, buddy!" he yelled. "That whole south thing is way overrated. The heat, the crowds—who needs it?" Sid took a deep breath as he fell into step with the mammoth, hurrying to keep pace. "Isn't this great?" he asked. "You and me, two of a kind . . . two bachelors knocking about in the wild—"

"No," Manfred broke in. "You just want a bodyguard so you don't become somebody's side dish."

With a smile, Sid nodded, slowing down. "You're a very shrewd mammal," he said, impressed.

Manfred didn't break his stride, and Sid had to run for a few moments to catch up again. "Okay, you lead the way, big fellow," the sloth wheezed cheerfully. "Mr. Big . . . I didn't catch the name—"

"*Manfred*," the mammoth supplied irritably.

"Manfred?" Sid replied. "Yuck. How about . . . Manny the moody mammoth? Manny the melancholy. . . Manny the—"

With a single blazing glare, Manfred cut off Sid's name games. Frightened, Sid scrambled up a nearby tree.

The mammoth wrapped his trunk around the tree, bending it toward him until he was face-to-face with

15

the sloth. "Stop following me!" Manfred ordered. Then he let go of the tree. It swayed wildly, shaking Sid.

Sid climbed down and followed Manfred on unsteady legs. "Okay, okay," Sid said, "so you've got issues. You won't even know I'm here. I'll just zip my lip—" He dragged his fingers across his lips like he was fastening a zipper.

Manfred didn't reply. He simply continued to trudge north.

Sid happily scurried along after him.

CHAPTER THREE

Not far from the river valley, a group of primitive human families had set up a campsite in a forest clearing near a cascading waterfall.

Male hunters dressed in skins and furs worked near the huts, repairing weapons and making tools. Women weaving baskets near the smoky fire kept their eyes on their children as they wove. A pack of domesticated wolves wandered through the campsite, nosing at the bones, tusks, and carcasses left over from earlier hunts.

In the middle of the camp, a baby named Roshan stood holding on to his father's leg. His father, Runar, was the leader of the human tribe. A few feet away, Nadia, Roshan's mother, held out her arms, urging him to walk to her. Roshan let go of his father's leg and tried to take a step. He stumbled and plopped down on his butt, giggling.

Unseen by the humans, two fierce-looking saber-toothed tigers watched the camp from their hiding spot on a hillside. They were both reddish-gold with long, sharp tusks protruding from their mouths.

"Oh, look at the cute little baby, Diego," the tiger named Soto growled to his companion. Soto, the leader of the pack, was larger and nastier-looking than Diego. "Isn't it nice he'll be joining us for breakfast?"

"It wouldn't be breakfast without him," Diego replied. He was awfully large and nasty-looking himself, and sleeker than Soto.

Soto glared down at the human settlement. "Especially since his daddy wiped out half our pack and wears our skin to keep warm." The tiger paced along a rocky outcropping on the hill. "An eye for an eye. Don't you think?"

Diego narrowed his golden eyes. "Let's show that human what happens when he messes with sabers."

"Alert the troops," Soto growled. "We attack at dawn."

Diego nodded and began to slink away.

"And, Diego, bring me that baby," Soto called. "Alive." A cruel light glittered in the muscular cat's eyes. "If I'm going to enjoy my revenge, I want it to be fresh."

––––––––––––

Above the river valley, densely packed stars sparkled in the inky sky. Manfred trudged through the landscape, carrying a huge load of branches on his tusks. He plodded between jagged peaks jutting into the darkness until he reached a sheltered depression in a hillside. There he dropped his pile of sticks, limbs, and leafy brush.

A few seconds later Sid waddled over, dragging a single dead branch behind him. "Whew!" Sid exclaimed. "I'm wiped out."

Manfred raised his bushy eyebrows at the lone stick Sid had gathered. "That's your shelter?"

"Hey," Sid replied. "You're a big guy—you got a lot of wood. I'm a little guy."

"You got half a stick."

Sid raised his branch in the air. "But with my little stick," he cried, "and my highly evolved brain—" The sloth accidentally poked himself in the eye with the stick. "Ow! I will create fire!"

"Fascinating," Manfred said as he turned to build his shelter.

"I've seen humans do it," Sid added. "How hard can it be?"

Manfred exhaled a soft snort through his trunk. "I've seen humans pick their noses," he shot back, "but it doesn't mean I'm gonna try it."

"We'll see if brains triumph over brawn tonight," Sid replied confidently.

A few hours later lightning flashed in the sky at the start of a downpour. Sid desperately rubbed two dripping sticks together. He was soaking wet.

Manfred watched from his snug lean-to a few feet away. He'd built the shelter across two giant boulders and it kept him perfectly dry. "Hey," he called to Sid sarcastically. "I think I saw a spark."

Sid walked over to Manfred's lean-to, hugging himself pathetically. "Any chance I could squeeze in there, Manny, ol' pal?"

"Isn't there someone else you can annoy?" Manfred asked. His huge bulk filled the shelter completely. "Friends, family, poisonous reptiles?"

"No," Sid answered. "My family abandoned me. They just . . . kinda migrated without me. You should see what they did last year. They woke up early and then they quietly tied my hands and feet and gagged me with a field mouse and barricaded the cave door and covered their tracks and went through water so I'd lose their scent and . . ." Sid trailed off, his voice dropping to a depressed whisper. "Ah, who needs them anyway?"

Sid tucked himself in under Manfred's trunk.

Manfred wrapped his trunk around Sid's neck. He picked up the sloth and deposited him on the wet ground outside the shelter.

"So, what about you?" Sid asked, propping up his head on his elbow. "You have family?"

Manfred heaved himself around in the lean-to, blocking the entrance with his gigantic rump.

"Okay," Sid said. "You're tired. We'll talk more in the morning."

Then it started to hail.

"Ouch!" Sid cried as he was pelted with the hard chunks of ice. "Ouch, ouch!" He scrambled closer to the shelter's entrance. "Uh, Manfred?" he asked weakly. "Manny? Could you skooch over a drop?"

Manfred didn't move.

"C'mon," Sid protested, "nobody falls asleep that fast." He waited for a response, but the mammoth remained still. "Manny?"

With a sigh Sid lifted Manfred's tail, and covered his head with it, hoping to get some sleep.

———————

Up the river from the valley, the fires in the human campsite sputtered out as the first fingers of dawn extended over the horizon.

Runar stretched as he woke. The chief rubbed the sleep from his eyes, stiffening when he heard the sound of running footsteps. Runar glanced up—and cried out in alarm. A pack of saber-toothed tigers was bounding down the slope toward his tribe.

Caught by surprise while sleeping, the humans were unprepared for the tiger attack. But they fought the tigers valiantly, their loyal wolves at their side.

Spear in hand, Runar battled the tigers, fending one off as he hurled his ivory boomerang at another. The boomerang zipped out and smashed a tiger on its skull, knocking it unconscious. Then the whirling weapon winged back to Runar's hand.

Diego slunk along the edge of the battle and slipped into Runar's tent. He immediately spotted the baby, Roshan. Diego grabbed the infant in his mouth and hurried outside.

When Runar saw Diego carrying Roshan, the chief's eyes opened wide with horror. He lunged toward Diego, but Soto leaped in Runar's path, cutting him off.

Diego glanced around the raging battle, trying to find the best way to escape the camp with the baby. He was just about to take off running when Nadia whacked him on the head with a sturdy club.

Dazed, Diego dropped the baby.

Nadia scooped up her son and dashed through the

campsite desperately. As she ran, her long black hair flew out behind her like a raven's wings.

Recovering quickly, Diego leaped to chase Nadia, snarling at her.

Nadia bolted up a long trail and hurried across a rope bridge that led to the top of a cliff. Diego followed. When she reached the cliff's edge, Nadia gazed in terror at the thundering waterfall crashing into the river below. She hugged Roshan tightly, quivering with panic.

From the campsite, Runar spotted his wife in trouble and started to run to help her. But Soto leaped into his path again, baring his sharp, bloody teeth.

Trapped on the edge of the cliff, Nadia tried to dart past Diego, but the tiger cut her off, forcing her back against the sheer drop. He stalked toward her slowly, intent on his mission of stealing the baby.

Nadia backed up. Her foot slipped on the rocky edge. As she recovered her balance, she peered down at the falls. Mist billowed up from the churning water far below.

Diego swiped out with his paw, trying to grab Roshan. His claw snagged the baby's necklace, flinging it behind him onto the bridge.

Nadia escaped the only way she could. She clasped her son to her chest and threw herself off the cliff. Diego watched as the woman and the baby plunged toward the churning water, disappearing into the thick veils of mist.

The battle at the campsite was still raging. Runar jabbed furiously at Soto with his spear as he tried to force the giant tiger out of his way. Soto lashed out with his claws, preventing the chief from running to his wife and son.

The tide of the battle turned as the humans and the wolves began to beat the tigers back. One human hunter speared the leg of a tiger named Lenny, and the chunky tiger let out a cry of pain as he backed away from the fight.

Soto spotted Diego running toward the tiger pack. "There's Diego!" Soto bellowed. "Fall back!"

The tigers immediately retreated from the campsite, with Lenny limping after them. As they ran from the humans, Soto fell into step beside Diego. "Where's the baby?" he panted.

"I lost it over the falls," Diego replied as he loped up a hillside.

Lenny and two other tigers named Oscar and Zeke groaned in irritation at Diego's announcement.

Soto shot Diego an enraged glare. "I want that baby!" he said, seething.

"I'll get it!" Diego replied.

Safely out of sight of the human camp, Soto cut

Diego off, stepping in front of him. "You'd better," the leader of the saber-toothed tigers hissed. "Unless you want to serve yourself as a replacement. We'll go up to Half-Peak volcano. Meet us there. And, Diego," Soto growled ominously, "you'd better hope it's alive."

_____

Above the human camp, Runar rushed up to the bridge that led to the cliff top. Searching around for a sign of his wife and son, he spotted the broken necklace that Diego had torn off Roshan. Runar picked it up and closed his fingers around it.

The other men of the tribe met Runar on his way back down the cliff. When they were all together, the chief pointed in the direction the tigers had fled, narrowing his eyes with determination.

The tribesmen nodded and then they set off to track down the saber-toothed tigers.

CHAPTER FOUR

"... **a**nd then she picks this hair off my shoulder," Sid prattled as he strolled along the riverbank with Manfred. "She says, 'If you're gonna have an extra mating dance, at least pick a female with the same color pelt.'"

Manfred stopped, glaring at Sid. "If you find a mate in life," the mammoth said sternly, "you should be loyal. Or in your case, *grateful*." Then he started lumbering along the river again. "Now get away from me."

As the mammoth walked off, Sid followed. "Well, I think mating for life is stupid," the sloth muttered.

"There's plenty of Sid to go around, you know."

With a bone-jarring thump, Sid bumped into the mammoth's leg. "Manny?" he asked, wondering why the mammoth had stopped short. When Manfred kept staring silently into the river, Sid crawled under the mammoth's stomach to check out the situation. As he came out between Manfred's front legs, his eyes widened. A human female was floating on her back, bobbing against the riverbank.

Roshan peeked from his blanket on top of Nadia's chest. He started to cry.

Manfred and Sid stared in amazement at the wet, frightened baby.

Sid shifted a little closer to the humans. He could see that Nadia was breathing, but she wasn't long for this world. She shivered and held Roshan close as her exhalations became ragged and painful.

Nadia's eyelids fluttered—she was slipping away. She gazed up at Manfred and then weakly placed her son on a rock, pushing Roshan toward the mammoth.

Manfred caught the baby with his trunk, stopping Roshan from slipping back into the water.

Nadia smiled. Her eyes filled with a grateful, peaceful expression.

As Manfred peered down at the baby, a dark shadow of sadness flickered across his face. His eyes brimmed with pain, as he seemed to be remembering something tragic.

"Look at that!" Sid said in an amazed voice, staring at the baby. "He's okay!"

Roshan smiled up at Sid.

Sid and Manfred both glanced back at the river.

The woman was gone. There were only ripples in the water where she had been floating.

Manfred turned around and trudged away.

"Hey, hey, hey, Manny!" Sid called. "Aren't you forgetting something?"

"No," Manfred replied. He kept walking.

Sid gaped at the departing mammoth, stunned. "But you just saved him . . ."

"I'm still trying to get rid of the last thing I saved," Manfred called.

"You can't just leave him here!" Sid hollered. The sloth hovered over Roshan, uncertain how to pick him up. Manfred was getting farther away, so Sid just grabbed the baby around the waist and hurried to catch up to the mammoth.

As Sid got closer, he pointed toward a nearby hilltop, where plumes of smoke were rising in streams. "Look, that's his herd up the hill. We should return him."

Manfred whirled around and leaned down to Sid. "Let's get something straight here," he said evenly.

"There is no *we*. There never *was* a we. In fact, without me, there wouldn't even be a *you*."

Sid smiled weakly. "Just up the hill?"

"Listen very carefully," Manfred said. He made sweeping gestures with his trunk to emphasize his next words. "I'm," he said, pointing at himself, "not . . ." The mammoth drew an "X" in the air. ". . . going!"

For a long moment Sid stared at Manfred, holding Roshan in his arms. Then he squared his fuzzy jaw. "Fine," he said. "Be a jerk. *I'll* take care of him."

"Yeah, that's good," Manfred replied sarcastically. "You can't even take care of yourself."

Ignoring the mammoth, Sid walked over to the rocky cliff and started climbing its steep slope.

"This I gotta see," Manfred whispered. He watched as Sid tried to scramble his way up. The sloth's awkward, squat, thick body wasn't built for climbing over rocks.

Sid nuzzled the top of Roshan's head. "I'll return you," he told the baby in a singsongy voice. "We don't need the meany-weeny mammoth, do we?"

"You're an embarrassment to nature," Manfred shouted. "You know that?"

"This is cake!" Sid called back. The truth was, he was already so tired that his legs wobbled under him and he was short of breath. He whispered faintly to himself, "*I'm gonna die. . . .*"

As Sid reached a boulder about twenty feet up the slope, the loose dirt gave way under his paws. He slipped. Roshan popped out of Sid's hands. The baby was airborne for a second, but then Sid kicked out and snagged Roshan's fur diaper with his toe. He began to lift the baby back to his hands. The fur diaper's stitching started to tear with a sickening *rip*.

"Manny!" Sid screamed.

The final threads in the stitching snapped.

Without thinking, Manfred rushed to catch Roshan as the baby plummeted straight for him.

An orange blur streaked out of nowhere and snatched Roshan from the air. Diego landed on a nearby rocky outcropping with the baby in his powerful jaws.

Panting around Roshan after his exhausting leap, Diego glanced up as an enormous shadow covered him. Before he could react, Manfred's trunk slammed him across the face with a stinging *slap*.

Roshan popped free and Manfred seized him.

"That pink thing is mine," Diego snarled.

"Ah, no," Sid called from the hillside. "Actually, it belongs to us."

Diego pawed at his jaw, checking it for damage. "*Us?*" the tiger asked, surprised. "You two are a bit of an odd couple."

"*There is no us,*" Manfred rumbled at Sid.

Sid moseyed down the slope. "Look," he told Diego as he passed him. "Sorry to interrupt your snack, but we've got to go."

"The baby?" Diego asked, as if surprised that Sid thought he wanted to eat Roshan. "Please. I was returning him to his herd."

Sid scoffed at that. "Yeah, nice try, bucktooth."

Abruptly, Diego leaped to Sid's side. "You calling me a *liar*?" he growled. His keen fangs glistened in the morning light.

"I . . . I . . ." Sid stuttered, gulping. "I didn't say that."

"You were thinking it," Diego replied.

Sid bustled over to Manfred. "I don't like this cat," he said. "He reads minds."

Diego shoved Sid out of the way so he could talk to Manfred. "Name's Diego, friend."

"Manfred," the mammoth introduced himself. "And I'm not your friend."

Diego took a step backward, baring his fangs. "Fine, *Manfred*," he snarled. "If you're looking for the humans, you're wasting your time. They left this morning."

"Thanks for the advice," Manfred replied. "Now beat it."

Keeping a wary eye on the tiger, Manfred leaned over to speak to Sid. "I'll help you bring it to its

31

herd," Manfred said, "but promise me you'll leave me alone after that." Then he turned and walked away.

"Okay," Sid replied, hurrying to follow the mammoth. "Deal. Fine." When Manfred didn't slow down, Sid called, "Hey, what's your problem?"

"*You* are my problem," the mammoth replied.

"Listen," Sid panted, finally catching up. "I don't want to make you self-conscious, but you ate four hundred pounds of food today. There's no way you need that much. Some of that has to be emotional."

"I have big bones," Manfred protested.

Sid smiled as he adjusted Roshan in his arms. "Hey, it's none of my business," he said, "but when you're ready to talk, I'm here."

Behind them, Diego glowered, his golden eyes glittering with intensity.

CHAPTER FIVE

Standing just below the top of the cliff, Sid raised Roshan in the air, holding him above the final ledge. Sid's plan was for the humans to see the baby, but not see him.

"What are you doing?" Manfred hissed from below. "Drop it on the ledge."

Sid placed Roshan onto the stone surface, and the baby scampered out of sight on his hands and knees.

"Should we make sure they found him?" Sid asked.

"Good idea," Manfred replied. He reached out his trunk toward Sid.

"No, wait—" Sid began before the mammoth tossed him over the ledge. The sloth screamed as he soared onto the high plateau.

Sid landed on his butt with a *plop*. He covered his eyes with his three-clawed paws, too terrified to look at the human settlement. "*Don't spear me!*" he yelped.

Roshan tugged the sloth's paw away from his face.

Peering around, Sid saw that he'd fallen in a grassy clearing. The human campsite was in another area a few yards away, past a grove of patchy trees. The camp appeared to be entirely empty. "Oh," Sid said. "This is a problem."

Manfred's head popped up over the ledge. "What now?" he asked. Then he got a good look at the deserted campsite. "Oh, that's *perfect*," the mammoth groused.

Nervously, Manfred and Sid wandered into the human settlement. The place looked like it had been abandoned in a hurry—there were still half-dismantled tents, straw beds, and cooking utensils lying about.

Roshan crawled over to a large woven basket. When he placed his hand on the edge, the basket flipped over, covering him. He started to crawl, turtle-like, toward a group of pallet beds.

Sid rushed to catch the crawling basket. He

ducked under a hanging clothesline and stepped on the tines of a rakelike tool, which popped up, bashing him in the face.

While Sid staggered around, dazed, Manfred watched Roshan crawling out from underneath the basket. The baby ambled over to a tiny straw bed— his bed—and patted it wistfully. Manfred inhaled, overwhelmed with sadness. Without his family, Roshan was truly alone.

"I told you they were gone," a voice growled.

Manfred turned to see Diego sauntering into the campsite. "Oh, look who it is," the mammoth said, rolling his eyes. "Don't you have some poor, defenseless animal to disembowel?"

Sid stumbled up to the mammoth and the tiger, searching the area for signs that showed where the humans had gone. "They couldn't be far," he said as he spotted footprints in the dirt. "They went this way," he decided, pointing north. Then he noticed tracks leading in the other direction. "Or this way," he said, scratching his head in confusion. "Or maybe . . . hmm. . . ."

"You don't know much about tracking, do you?" Diego sneered.

Sid shrugged. "Hey, I'm a sloth," he replied. "See a tree, eat a leaf—that's my tracking."

Diego loped over to Manfred. "Look, you didn't

miss them by much," the tiger explained. He showed the mammoth a broken branch on a bush. "It's still green," he said. "They headed north two hours ago."

Behind the tiger, Sid stuck two pieces of twig into his mouth like saber teeth. "Still green," he imitated Diego. "They left two hours ago."

Roshan giggled at the sloth. The baby sat down on a large wooden spoon, which catapulted a dead fish onto Manfred's face. Roshan cackled with laughter.

Diego shook his head. "You don't need this aggravation," he told the mammoth. "Give me the baby. I can track humans down a lot faster than you can."

Manfred brushed the fish off his face and peered down at Diego suspiciously. "And you're just a good citizen helping out, right?"

Casually swaying his tail, Diego pretended to be nonchalant. "I just know where the humans are going."

"Glacier Pass," Manfred said. The mammoth shrugged when Diego looked startled. "Everybody knows they have a settlement on the other side."

Diego covered up his surprise. "Well, unless you know how to track," he said, "you're never gonna reach them before the pass closes up with snow. Which should be, like . . . tomorrow."

The mammoth tapped the tip of his trunk against his lips, thinking it over.

"So you can give that baby to me," Diego continued smoothly, "or go get lost in a blizzard. Your choice."

Manfred glanced at Sid.

Sid grinned his wide, goofy smile and waved.

After picking up Roshan, Manfred took a step toward Diego. Manfred held out Roshan toward the tiger . . . and at the last second changed his mind, stuffing the baby into Sid's muddy arms. "Here's your little bundle of joy," Manfred told Sid gruffly. "We're returning it to the humans."

Sid smiled and hugged Roshan. "Aw, the big, bad, tigey-wigey gets left behind," he taunted Diego, patting the tiger's muzzle. "Aw, poor tigey-wigey—"

"Sid?" Manfred interrupted. "Tigey-wigey's gonna lead the way."

Sid gulped and snatched his hand away from Diego. Then he faced the mammoth. "Uh . . . Manny, can I talk to you for a second?"

"No," Manfred replied. "The sooner we find the humans, the sooner I get rid of Mr. Stinky Drool Face . . . and the baby." With that, Manfred shambled off, heading north.

Diego slowly circled Sid. "You won't always have Jumbo around to protect you," the tiger whispered menacingly. "And when that day comes, I suggest you watch your back . . . 'cause I'll be chewing on it."

Sid gulped again and wrapped his arms protectively around Roshan. "Help me," he whispered to himself.

"Hey, Mr. Expert Tracker," Manfred called to Diego, "up front where I can see you."

Diego sprinted down the trail ahead of Manfred, leading the way.

With a big sigh, Sid waddled nervously after them, already lagging behind.

As the sun set that evening, the sound of Roshan's wailing echoed across the long, flat plateau that Sid, Manfred, and Diego were crossing. Sid held the screaming baby in his arms

"You gotta make it stop," Manfred moaned, pulling up to a halt. "I can't take it anymore."

"I've eaten things that didn't complain this much!" Diego added.

Sid tried to comfort Roshan, but he just cried louder. "It won't stop squirming."

"You're holding it wrong," Diego informed Sid. "Just put it down."

Sid lowered Roshan toward the ground head-first.

"Watch its head!" Manfred instructed.

"Sheesh!" Sid complained. "Pick him up, put him down. Make up your mind already!"

Diego padded over to Roshan and bumped the

baby's nose with his own. "Its nose is dry," Diego informed the others.

"That means something's wrong with it," Sid said.

"Someone should lick it just in case," Diego suggested.

Sid raised his hand, volunteering happily. "I'll do it!" The sloth kneeled beside Roshan and stuck out his tongue, ready to lick the baby.

"Hey," Manfred said, interrupting Sid. The mammoth pointed toward Roshan's fur diaper with his trunk. "He's wearing one of those baby-thingies."

"*Tho?*" Sid asked in a lisp, his tongue still hanging out.

"So if he poops," Manfred replied, "where does it go?"

Instantly, Sid's tongue zipped back into his mouth. "Humans are disgusting." He groaned.

Roshan took a deep breath and let out another wail, even louder than before.

"Okay," Manfred said. He nudged Sid with his trunk. "You. Check for poop."

Sid narrowed his eyes. "Why am I the poop checker?"

Manfred let out a loud snort. "Because returning the runt was your idea," he replied, "and because you're small and insignificant. And because I'll pummel you if you don't."

ide, goofy smile crossed Sid's face. "Why

n the ground, Roshan kept crying louder and
ier, sobbing fire-engine wails.

"Now, Sid!" Manfred insisted.

Sid nodded. He turned his face away as far as his neck would twist, then started to remove Roshan's fur diaper with a shaking hand. "Eew . . . yuck," Sid gasped. "Eew! I mean, my goodness!" Sid slid the pelt off Roshan and stood up, waving the fur diaper in the air. "Yuck!" he cried. He took a step toward Manfred. "Look out, coming through!" Sid shouted.

"Watch out!" Manfred hollered, cringing at the sight of the diaper.

Sid turned, stumbling on purpose toward Diego.

"Stop waving that thing around!" Diego screeched as he jumped away.

Staggering, Sid wobbled on his feet, shoving the diaper closer to Diego. Then Sid tripped over his own gawky feet, just as he turned around again to face Manfred.

The diaper launched into the air and landed with a wet smack on the mammoth's face.

"Eew!" Manfred bellowed. "Yuck!"

Sid rolled on the ground, laughing hysterically. "Ah-ha!" he cried. "Got you! It's clean." Still laughing, the sloth pulled himself to his feet and picked up the crying baby.

Manfred bopped Sid on the head with his trunk.

While the sloth was seeing stars, Roshan stopped sobbing and giggled for a second.

All the animals froze, staring at the baby. But then Roshan began to wail again.

With a firm whack, Manfred bopped Sid on the head a second time.

Roshan giggled again.

"Hey, keep doing that," Diego told Manfred. "He likes it!"

Manfred smacked Sid. "Yeah," the mammoth said cheerfully. "And it's making me feel better, too!"

Sid held out Roshan to Diego. "Here," he said woozily. "You hold him."

This time Diego swiped out a paw and bashed Sid on the head.

Roshan chortled happily. Then the baby raised a teeny fist and bopped Sid a good one, giggling. Roshan got ready to hit Sid again, but the sloth grabbed his little hand, stopping him. Instantly, the baby began to scream and cry once more.

"Here, turn him toward me," Diego said in a frustrated voice. As Sid put Roshan down on the ground, Diego bumped the sloth out of the way. Then the tiger leaned over until he was face-to-face with the baby. He clenched his sharp teeth together and hid his eyes with his paws. "Where's the baby?" Diego gurgled in the most terrifying game of peek-aboo ever. He uncovered his eyes and lunged toward Roshan with his sharp teeth gleaming. "*There he is!*"

Roshan howled loud, frightened sobs.

Manfred shoved Diego out of the way and grabbed the baby in his trunk. "Stop it," the mammoth scolded. "You're scaring him."

The baby's stomach rumbled loudly.

"I bet he's hungry," Sid said.

"How about some milk?" Manfred asked.

Sid rubbed his stomach. "I'd love some!"

"Not you," Diego hissed. "The baby."

Sid put his hands on his hips, looking offended. "I ain't exactly lactating right now, pal," he replied.

With a growl, Diego leaped very close to the sloth. "You're a little low on the food chain to be mouthing off, aren't you?"

"Enough!" Manfred bellowed. His loud command echoed across the plateau, bouncing off the walls of a faraway canyon.

As the sound faded away, the animals suddenly noticed a single ripe green melon nestled on the ground beside some bushes.

"Food!" they cheered.

Manfred rushed over to the melon and picked it up. Instantly, a funny-looking flightless bird ran up to the mammoth. It was a dodo bird—sort of like a little penguin with a dopey face and a large beak. The dodo snatched the melon off Manfred's trunk and hurried away, dribbling the round fruit between its feet like a soccer ball.

"*Bakaak!*" the dodo squawked. "*Bakaak bakaak!*"

The dodo bustled around a rocky formation, disappearing from sight. Manfred, Diego, and Sid stared at one another in amazement for a long moment.

Then they chased after it.

CHAPTER SIX

As Sid, Manfred, and Diego followed the dodo around the corner, they saw a very strange sight: a dodo military compound, filled with the flightless birds preparing for the Ice Age.

A line of marching dodos filed past a sergeant on a wooden perch. "I don't know but I've been told!" the sergeant shouted.

"I don't know but I've been told!" the marching dodos repeated.

"End of the world be mighty cold!" the sergeant yelled.

"End of the world be mighty cold!" the training dodos called back. One of the marching dodos in the front of the line tripped and fell on the ground. He was stomped flat by the marchers behind him.

Across the compound, another group of dodos were in basic training—jumping, ducking under obstacles, and trying unsuccessfully to fly. Overseeing the training were a corporal and two motivational speakers. The three overseers were perched on a tall platform high above the compound.

"Prepare for the Ice Age!" one of the motivational speakers intoned.

"Protect the dodo way of life!" the other added.

The corporal raised his baton. "Survival separates the dodo from the beast!" he cried, swinging the baton enthusiastically. The baton smacked into one of the motivational speakers beside him, knocking him off the platform.

Sid carried Roshan into the compound, followed closely by Manfred and Diego. They watched as the dodo that they'd first seen put down his melon on a stump beside two other melons.

Sid pointed to the dodo that had carried the melon. "You see?" he said to his companions loudly. "I told you he went this way!"

"Prepare for the Ice Age!" the remaining speaker called from his perch.

"Ice Age?" Sid whispered in confusion.

Diego rolled his golden eyes. "I've heard of these crackpots," he said.

The dodo they'd followed gasped when he spotted the sloth, the baby, the mammoth, and the tiger. "*Bakaak!*" the dodo screeched. "Intruders!"

He rushed deeper into the compound toward a group of dodos standing by a pit of boiling water.

"Now don't fall in," a dodo named Dorn told the others standing next to him. "If you do, you will definitely—"

The dodo that had carried the melon ran up to them. "Intruders!" he hollered, interrupting the stirring dodo. "Intru—" He tripped and plunged into the boiling pit with a scream, disappearing from sight.

Dorn stared down in the pit. "—burn and die," he finished.

Manfred approached the dodos beside the pit. "Guys," he called, "can we have our melon back?" He pointed with his trunk toward Roshan, who Sid had set down on the ground. "Junior's hungry."

"No way," another dodo named Dab replied, putting his hands on his hips. "This is our private stockpile for the Ice Age. Subarctic temperatures will force us underground for a million billion years."

The mammoth raised his bushy eyebrows. "So you got three melons?"

"If you weren't smart enough to plan ahead," Dab scolded Manfred, "then doom on you!"

"Doom on you!" all the dodos in the compound muttered. Their voices rose to a loud chant as they marched in step toward Manfred. "Doom on you, doom on you!"

"Get away from me!" Manfred hollered.

To protect one of the melons, Dab threw himself on top of it. The melon shot out from under him and sailed right into Roshan's arms.

"Oh, no!" Dab screamed. "No! Retrieve the melon!" He raised a fist in the air. "Tae kwon dodos, attack!"

Three dodos dressed in martial arts robes stepped out from behind trees. They chopped the air with their hands. "*Hi-yah!*" they grunted, kicking into the air and approaching Roshan. The tae kwon dodos wrestled the melon away from Roshan. "Here!" one of them yelled. "Quick!" He hurled the melon to a dodo behind him. The dodo caught it, then pitched it to another. The next dodo tossed the melon over his shoulder. But there were no more dodos behind him. The melon sailed over the edge of the cliff.

"The melon! The melon!" all the dodos screamed.

They rushed after it, following it straight over the cliff.

Meanwhile, Sid grabbed one of the two remaining melons from the tree stump. Before he could get a firm hold on it, three more dodos jumped him and pulled the melon back. They played keep-away with it, tossing the melon over Sid's head.

With a short jump, Sid managed to swat the melon away from them. It sailed toward the pit of boiling water.

The dodos chased after the melon and managed to catch it with their beaks. A second later they lost their balance and tumbled into the boiling water, the melon right behind them.

The remaining dodos turned and saw the last melon on the tree stump. They jumped on it, trying to grab it, but ended up in a ball of confusion. The melon rolled away. Manfred caught it with his trunk and began to carry it toward Roshan. But four of the dodos noticed what he was doing, and they rushed him. For a few moments Manfred simply held the melon high above their heads as the dodos tried to jump at it.

Another dodo had the bright idea of slamming into Manfred's wide behind. With a startled cry, Manfred couldn't help launching the melon into the air.

The bruised fruit plopped down near three other dodos. It bounced off the head of one, knocking him down, bounced to the next, knocking him down, and bounced off the third and right into Sid's arms.

A throng of dodos surrounded Sid, leaving him nowhere to run. He decided to charge straight into them, knocking them down like bowling pins. A bunch of the birds flew up in the air, then landed one on top of the other in a teetering tower that looked like an enormous totem pole. The rest of the dodos closed in on Sid. He leaped triumphantly over their heads, landing in the clear and skidding to a halt right in front of Manfred, Diego, and Roshan, who all cheered. Sid raised the melon over his head, doing a jiggy end-zone dance. Overcome by excitement, he spiked the melon hard onto the ground.

It smashed with a *splat*.

"Aw, Sid!" Manfred groaned. "Now we gotta find more food."

But Roshan didn't care if the melon was squished—he began to chow down on it happily, smearing soggy melon juice all over his face.

"More to the right!" a dodo frantically ordered from behind them. "More to the right!" With heavy footsteps, the leaning tower of dodos wobbled toward the animals.

But the dodos weren't very good at steering. The

tower lurched toward the edge of a cliff. Plunging off the ledge, the dodos screamed in terror as they dropped out of sight.

"Hey, look at that," Manfred said, sounding amused. "Dinner and a show."

Diego shook his head at the pitiful defenses of the dodos. "I give that species forty thousand years, tops."

CHAPTER SEVEN

Later that evening, after walking for the rest of the day, the four travelers settled in for a peaceful sleep in a bushy section of the mountainside. The sky was moonlit and clear, and Sid nodded off, listening to soothing insect and animal calls in the distance.

Manfred blinked sleepily. He had Roshan curled up loosely in his trunk. The mammoth tried to keep watch over Diego, who was sleeping close by, but he just couldn't stay awake any longer.

As soon as Manfred drifted off, Diego popped open his golden eyes. He got up and padded silently toward Roshan.

A twig snapped in the thick bushes nearby.

Diego whipped around to look. Then he froze, holding his ears rigid and alert.

But he didn't see anything, and the night faded back to silence . . . except for Sid's snoring.

Manfred's trunk unfurled a bit more as he slipped deeper into slumber.

Sneaking closer, Diego saw that he could snatch Roshan out of Manfred's trunk if he was careful enough. He took a few more steps until he was only a foot away.

Another twig snapped in the underbrush nearby.

Without waking up, Manfred curled up his trunk more tightly around Roshan.

Diego's eyes glittered with annoyance. He slunk low to the ground, his ears pinned back against his skull as he snuck toward the bushes.

The second Diego heard leaves rustling in the underbrush, he pounced.

He landed on a tiger hiding in the bushes. Diego tackled the tiger, a sharp claw raised above the big cat's throat.

"Go ahead," the tiger growled. "Slice me. It'll be the last thing you ever do." It was crazy Zeke, a tiger from Diego's own pack.

"I'm working here, you waste of fur," Diego snarled.

"Frustrated, Diego?" another tiger asked.

Diego whirled around and came face-to-face with Oscar, who had snuck up behind him.

A smirk played on Oscar's lips. "Tracking down helpless infants too difficult for you?" He sneered.

"What are you two doing here?" Diego asked.

Oscar swished his tail. "Soto's getting tired of waiting."

"Yeah," Zeke added. "He said come back with the baby or don't come back at all."

Diego stepped away from Zeke and started to walk up the slope of the hill through the bushes. Then he turned around suddenly, his eyes flashing with cold rage. "I have a message for Soto," he said. "Tell him I'm bringing the baby. And tell him I'm bringing . . . a *mammoth*."

Oscar blinked at Diego in surprise. "Mammoths never travel alone."

"Well, this one does," Diego replied. "And I'm leading him to Half-Peak."

Zeke and Oscar followed Diego as he led them closer to his sleeping traveling companions. Zeke started to drool as soon as he saw Manfred. "Mmm, look at all that meat," he said, hissing. "Let's get him!" He leaped forward.

Diego yanked Zeke back roughly. "No!" he insisted. "Not yet. We'll need the whole pack to bring this mammoth down. Get everyone ready."

The instant Diego released Zeke, he bounded

away to tell the other tigers, and Oscar quickly followed.

As soon as they were gone, Diego padded back to where Sid, Roshan, and Manfred slept.

He curled up next to them and settled down for the night.

———————

The morning was misty. Puffy white clouds surrounded the base of the mountain, turning pastel colors as the sun rose.

Manfred stretched sleepily as he awoke. He blinked his eyes and looked down at his trunk.

Roshan was gone!

The mammoth hurried over to where Diego had settled to sleep. Diego leaped to his feet when Manfred approached.

"Where's the baby?" Manfred demanded.

"What do you mean, where's the baby?" the tiger asked, his voice gravelly with panic. "You lost it?"

They glanced around, confused for a moment. Then, at the same time, they both realized who had taken the baby.

"*Sid*?" they yelled together.

Sid wasn't too far away. Near a group of tall, skinny rock formations, he had found a muddy hot-spring pool. He was reclining in the pool with Roshan on his lap. Two attractive lady sloths named Jennifer and Rachel were also in the pool.

"*Ooo,*" Rachel gushed, staring at Roshan with her big blue eyes. "It's so ugly, it's positively adorable!"

Jennifer waved her fingers at the baby. "Hello, pumpkin," she cooed fondly. A tall question mark of white hair stuck up from the top of her head, bobbing as she spoke. "Little baldy bean . . ."

"Where did you find it?" Rachel asked.

Sid hugged Roshan on his lap. "Poor kid," the sloth replied. "All alone in the wild . . . sabers were closing in . . . so, I snatched him."

"So brave," Rachel breathed, impressed.

"Well, he needed me," Sid said modestly. "I only wish I had one of my own."

Jennifer shifted closer to Sid in the natural hot tub. "Really?" she asked. "I find that attractive in a male."

"Who *wouldn't* want a family, I always say," Sid added.

Rachel began to rub Sid's shoulders. "Where have you been hiding?"

Sid blushed. "Well . . . you know," he mumbled.

With a cheerful gurgle, Roshan chucked a handful of mud into Sid's face.

Spluttering, Sid wiped off his eyes. "Cute kid," he said. He reached for something to dry off with and grabbed a sturdy mammoth trunk instead. "So, uh . . .

as I was saying . . ." Then Sid paused, realizing what he had in his hands. He peered up and saw Manfred glaring down at him.

Sid let out a scared chuckle. "Hi, Manny."

Manfred bopped Sid with his trunk and then took Roshan away from the sloth. "What's the *matter* with you?" he growled as he turned and strode away.

"Uh . . . can I talk to you a sec?" Sid called after Manfred. The sloth climbed out of the muddy pool. "Excuse us, ladies. You just keep marinating, and I'll be right back."

Sid rushed to catch up to Manfred. "No, no, no," he pleaded. "Wait, wait, wait, I'm begging you. I *need* him."

"What?" Manfred asked sarcastically. "A good-looking guy like you?"

"You say that," Sid said, lowering his head, "but you don't really mean it."

Manfred stared at the sloth through narrowed eyes. "No, seriously, look at you," he continued, his voice sounding angry. "Aw, those ladies don't stand a chance."

Biting his lip, Sid hugged himself with his long, hairy arms. "You have a very cruel sense of humor."

"Hey," Manfred replied with a shrug, "don't let us cramp your style."

Misunderstanding the mammoth, Sid's face split with a goofy grin. He reached for the baby. "Thanks,

Manny, you're a pal!" he gushed. "You're the best!"

But before Sid could take Roshan, Manfred pulled the baby away and walked off with him. "Without Pinky," the mammoth added.

"Manny, Manny!" Sid cried. "I need him!"

But Manfred had already stalked away.

Sid shrugged and glanced back toward the mud bath. It was shrouded in steam. He hurried over to it, strutting like he was the coolest sloth in the world. "So," Sid said as he hopped in. "Where were we?"

But the lady sloths were gone.

As the mist cleared, Sid could see that on either side of him was a rhinoceros. Frank on his left, Carl on his right. They did not look happy to see him.

———————

"A pretty tail walks by," Manfred groused about Sid as he wandered back toward their campsite, "and suddenly he moves like a cheetah!"

Roshan giggled as he swung in the mammoth's trunk.

"And that tiger," Manfred continued. "Yeah, Mr. Great Tracker. He can't even find a sloth."

Manfred came to a stop near a tall tree. He plopped Roshan down on a branch.

"What am I, their wet nurse?" the mammoth complained.

Up on the branch, Roshan cooed sweetly, enjoying the view. He waved down at Manfred.

Manfred poked him with the tip of his trunk. "What are you looking at, bonebag?" the mammoth asked. "You're supposed to grow into a great predator? I don't think so."

Playfully, Roshan tried to grab Manfred's trunk with his hands, but the mammoth moved his elongated nose out of reach.

"You're just a little patch of fur," Manfred said. He opened Roshan's mouth and peered inside. "No fangs," he noted. He raised the thick fringe of the baby's hair. "No horns." Then he picked Roshan up off the branch and flipped him upside down. "You're folds of skin wrapped in . . . mush. What's so threatening about you?"

Roshan reached out and grabbed Manfred's trunk. He squealed in triumph, then pressed his cheek to the trunk and hugged it.

A soft expression misted Manfred's eyes for a moment. But then the mammoth remembered to act tough and he pulled away. "Hey, does this look like a petting zoo?" he growled, putting Roshan back on the branch.

With a quick hand motion, Roshan yanked out a hunk of Manfred's nose hair.

"Ow!" Manfred cried.

Roshan laughed. He threw the nose hair up in the air. It rained on him like confetti.

"All right, wise guy," Manfred scolded. "You just earned yourself a timeout." He used his trunk's tip as a suction cup, clinging to the top of Roshan's head. The mammoth deposited the baby upside down on a higher tree limb.

Roshan chortled, enjoying the reversed aerial view of the world, clapping his hands. Manfred's hairy face looked particularly silly upside down.

"Oh, you think that's funny?" Manfred asked. "How about this?" He wedged Roshan onto the highest branch on the tree, as far as his long trunk could reach. "Now who's laughing?" Manfred called. "You'll be a little snack for the owls."

But the height didn't bother the baby at all. Roshan clapped his hands again, laughing at the pleasurable breeze through the treetops.

"You're a brave little squirt," Manfred said. "I'll give you that."

———————

"Sidney?" a chirpy female voice called.

Sid's eyes popped open, wide with fear. "Oh, no." He moaned. He recognized that voice. It belonged to Sylvia, who he had last seen being dragged away by migrating glyptodons.

"Sidney, is that you?" Sylvia screeched.

Struggling to his feet from where the rhinos had trampled him into the mud, Sid prepared to run for it. But Sylvia hurried over and leaped at him. She landed on his back, knocking him over, smashing his face into the dirt again.

"Sidney, what happened?" Sylvia babbled. "Did you get lost? Did you get eaten? You don't look eaten."

"I—" Sid gasped.

"It's been two days," Sylvia continued. "I couldn't find you anywhere."

Sid scooted out from under her and sat up. "Because I was attacked!" he explained. "By two . . . two *hundred* vicious rhinos!"

Concerned, Sylvia reached out to him with her paw. "Oh, Sidney, are you okay?" she gushed. "That's horrible!"

Sid gently pushed her hand away. "I survived," he replied.

Sylvia smiled hopefully at him. "Then are you ready to migrate?"

"Yes, I am!" Sid lied, hopping to his feet. He thought quickly, trying to invent an excuse to escape. "Once I get your turnips!"

"My *turnips*?" Sylvia asked, confused.

"Sure!" Sid replied. "We're going to have to stuff our cheeks if we're going to migrate all those miles."

The Ice Age is coming! It all began with a little scrat.

Sid offers Frank and Carl a pinecone after ruining their lunchtime salad.

Manny saves Sid from being trampled by two very angry rhinos.

Nadia entrusts her baby, Roshan, to Manfred and Sid. ⬇

At first, Manny makes it clear he's not going anywhere with Sid. ↓

Roshan comes face to tooth with Diego.

Sid gets to be the poop checker.

Diego finds a chance to steal Roshan and take him to Soto. ⬆

Sid impresses his new friends, Jennifer and Rachel, with a mud-covered Roshan. ⬆

Everybody run! It's an avalanche! ⬇

Ahhh! Sid gets left behind in the ice cave.

Uh-oh! Where's Roshan going?

Sid saves the day!

After their slippery ride, the herd ends up in a cave covered with mysterious paintings. ⬆

The herd learns about Manfred's family.

Roshan takes his first steps—right toward Diego! ⬇

Father and son, together at last. ⬆

Sylvia batted her eyelashes at him and exhaled dreamily, very pleased with his planning. "Oh, *Sidney.*"

"I'll just run!" Sid chirped. He took a few steps away from the lady sloth. "And get them!" He loped around the corner of a tall mesa as fast as his slow-motion legs would carry him.

And ran smack into Diego's face.

"Oh!" Sid cried. "Thank goodness you're here!"

As Diego watched suspiciously, Sid scrunched up his face in a fake terrified expression. "Oh, no!" he screamed, loudly enough for Sylvia to hear around the corner. "A tiger! *Help!*"

"Where's the baby?" Diego growled.

"He's fine," Sid whispered. "Manfred has him. Come on, roar. *Roar!*"

"Meow," Diego replied in a bored voice.

This wasn't exactly what Sid had in mind.

"He just ate a cat!" Sid cried to Sylvia. "Now he's coming for me! Oh, no! He's got me! Oh, help!"

Diego pulled away from Sid, extremely annoyed. "Get *away* from me."

"I'm coming, Sid!" Sylvia hollered from around the mesa. "Hold on!"

With Diego refusing to play along, and Sylvia coming around the corner any second, Sid got desperate. He grabbed the tiger's paw and bit it—hard.

Diego roared in pain.

Sid dove into the tiger's open mouth and hung there limply . . . just as Sylvia showed up.

"Oh!" Sylvia gasped. "Sid!"

"Sylvia," Sid moaned, covering his forehead with his paw. "I . . . I love you."

Then Sid stiffened, faking death. He let himself droop floppily in Diego's mouth, lolling his head.

After a long moment, Sid peeked to check her reaction. Sylvia was staring right at him, so he quickly squeezed his eyes shut.

"I can see you breathing," Sylvia said flatly.

Sid inhaled, holding it so his chest wouldn't heave up and down.

"Now you're holding your breath," Sylvia said.

With a loud groan, Sid exhaled a painful-sounding death rattle from the back of his throat. He shuddered and then lay still, trying to fake death again.

Sylvia glared at him, her face twitching with disgust. She tightened her claws to fists and looked directly into Diego's golden eyes.

"Eat him," she told the tiger.

CHAPTER EIGHT

When Sylvia stormed away, Sid stopped playing dead. "Oh, I hate to break their hearts," the sloth said insincerely.

Diego's eyes glistened with a hard, hungry glint.

"All right . . . thanks," Sid said. "You can put me down now."

Diego didn't move. Sid gulped nervously.

"Sylvia!" Sid screamed, panic making his voice harsh. "*Sylvia!*"

For a long, tense moment, Sid wasn't sure what was going to happen. Then Manfred's huge shadow flowed around the corner. "Let's get moving before the pass closes," he said.

go spat Sid out and the sloth landed on the ground in a damp heap.

"Boy," Sid said, brushing himself off. "For a second there I actually thought you were going to eat me."

Diego raised his muzzle in disdain. "I don't eat junk food," he replied. Then the tiger turned and followed Manfred away from the rocky outcropping. A light snowfall began to flutter down from the sky.

Diego led the others through the valley. They followed a long, muddy path for miles alongside the sheer face of a gigantic glacier. Heading north, they marched for the rest of the day, until it was cold enough for all of them to see their breath in clouds of white vapor.

Roshan rode high on the mammoth's back, while Diego hurried ahead, examining a trail of human and tiger tracks that only he could identify. Sid lagged behind wearily.

Diego leaped up on a stack of rocks to get a clear view. He twitched his nose in an uneasy gesture as he scanned the landscape. Runar and the other humans were marching single-file through the valley below.

The tiger glanced over his shoulder. Manfred was trudging closer with Sid not far behind. Desperate for them not to see the humans, Diego glanced around and noticed a jagged crevice—an opening in the massive glacier's wall. It was partially hidden under an overhanging canopy of ice, which curved over a large space like a frozen tidal wave. Diego jumped down off the rocks before the mammoth could get any closer.

"Hey, great news," Diego reported cheerfully. "I found a shortcut."

Atop Manfred, Roshan banged his fists on the mammoth's broad back, amusing himself.

"Ow," Manfred said, glaring up at the baby. Then he turned back to face Diego. "What do you mean, *shortcut*?"

"I mean, faster than the longer way around," Diego replied.

"I know what a shortcut is," Manfred snapped.

"Look," Diego said, nodding his head toward the crevice in the glacier wall. "Either we slip through there and beat the humans to Glacier Pass or we go the long way and miss them."

Manfred ducked his head to see under the icy canopy and warily inspected the ragged hole. "Through there?" he asked. His hulking body would barely squeeze through the crevice—if it fit at all. "What do you take me for?"

"This time tomorrow," Diego replied, "you could be a free mammoth."

"Hey, guys!" Sid called. "Check it out!" The sloth

sauntered up to Diego and Manny. He had broken an icicle in half and now held a piece to each side of his neck, giving the illusion that he'd been impaled. He staggered, pretending to gasp and gurgle.

Manfred rolled his big eyes at the ridiculous sloth and pointed at the hole in the ice. "Sid," he called. "The tiger found a shortcut."

Sid gazed up at the towering glacier above the crevice. Its height was dizzying, the very top disappearing into faraway clouds. "No, thanks," he said. "I choose life." He turned around and continued along the trail, striding closer to the spot where Diego had looked down into the valley.

Diego zipped in front of the sloth, cutting him off. "Then I suggest you take the shortcut," he snarled.

Sid blinked at the tiger suspiciously. "Are you threatening me?"

"*Move*, sloth!" Diego roared.

The tiger's exasperated, thundering bellow echoed through the mountains, rumbling and vibrating along their overloaded caps of snow. The reverberations shattered the vast ice crust and the colossal frozen sheet crumbled, tumbling down the mountains in a howling avalanche.

"Way to go, tiger," Sid complained as the churning mass of snow careened straight toward them.

Diego whirled around and bared his sharp fangs

at the sloth. But instead of swiping a paw at Sid's head, he shouted, "Quick! Inside!" when he saw the approaching avalanche.

They ran under the glacier's overhanging canopy near the crevice. Just as they reached safety, the avalanche hit in a thundering cascade. The over-hang shook violently as the snow pummeled its curved roof. Sid glanced up at the ceiling of the icy shelter and gulped in terror. Long, sharp icicles dangled overhead, wobbling dangerously. The animals huddled together, expecting to be pierced by icicles at any moment. Roshan held on tightly to Manfred's fur, burying his face in the mammoth's back.

The roar of the avalanche suddenly stopped. It was over in an instant as the snow settled. The icicles remained where they were.

The trio glanced at the spot where they had entered the cavelike space to escape the avalanche. A thirty-foot wall of snow now blocked their exit to the outside world. The crack in the glacier offered the only possible path.

"Okay," Manfred said. "I vote shortcut."

A few minutes later, in the tunnel beyond the crevice, the animals slowly made their way between enormous, strangely sculpted blocks of ice. Sunlight filtered weakly through the frozen mountain, spattering random beams and fractured, shadowy designs on the path.

As Diego led the way, the glacier creaked and groaned under its own weight. Cracks in the ice rang out like gunshots, causing spiderweb patterns to appear on the frozen surfaces.

"C'mon, guys," Diego called as he turned a corner, his voice echoing. "Stick together. It's easy to get lost in here."

Manfred and Sid rushed to catch up to the tiger. As soon as they rounded the bend in the tunnel, they were greeted by a dazzling natural display. They stared in awe at the forest of thin icicles extending from floor to ceiling in the wide chamber. The icicles looked incredibly delicate, like strands of hand-blown glass. The sound of slowly dripping water added a spooky atmosphere to the beautiful room.

Gaping in amazement, Sid paid no attention to where he was walking. He bashed his forehead on a low-hanging icicle and fell to the floor, dazed.

"Hey, guys," he called out. Sid's eyes widened when he noticed something staring at him from behind the ice. "Ahhh," he started to yell. Then he realized it was only a fish frozen in the ice and continued on his way. He turned and entered a long corridor.

On the corridor's wall, a huge, snarling dinosaur

was encased in the ice. Sid shuddered and looked around for his companions. He spotted them ahead and hurried to catch up, stopping only briefly to study a series of frozen amoebalike blobs that resembled the evolution of a sloth that looked just like Sid. When he reached Manfred and Diego, they were passing a silvery, saucer-shaped UFO trapped in the frozen wall.

Manfred glanced at Sid with an annoyed expression. "Will you keep up, please?" he scolded, passing under a low, icy shelf. "It's hard enough to keep track of *one* baby."

Roshan crawled off Manfred's back and scampered onto the overhanging ledge. He giggled happily as he explored. At the rear of the ledge was a sleek slope. Roshan pushed himself onto the ice slide and instantly zipped down it.

The baby shot past the others into another slick tunnel, whizzing out of sight. The animals took off after him. They had only taken a few steps before stumbling onto a broad slide of their own. They slipped down, gushing into a huge pipe of ice. They zoomed off in different directions, whipping, bouncing, and careening through sleek frozen funnels as though they were on a gigantic roller coaster. Up ahead, Roshan *whooshed* through a steep bend, gliding on his fur diaper and laughing with glee.

Sid shrieked as he spotted a glittering wall of ice directly ahead of him. He smashed through it, barely slowing down. A second later Diego and Manfred plowed through the same wall.

The sloth, hurtling down the slide on his sleek fur, began to catch up to Roshan. He reached down between his paws to grab the baby.

Right when Sid snagged Roshan, they reached a protruding ice ramp off to the side of the chute. Sid went one way, Roshan went another.

Manfred slid by them as he surged through a curved tunnel sideways. "Yeow!" the mammoth bellowed.

Diego screamed as he shot off an ice ledge into empty space. The tiger clawed at the air, tumbling down a short vertical pipe.

Sid blasted out of a tight tunnel like a cannonball, smacking onto Manfred's shoulder. The sloth grunted and grabbed hold of the mammoth's tusks. Using them as handlebars, Sid steered around ice boulders as the two of them barreled down a slide.

Yowling, Diego zoomed out of a chute and landed on Manfred's rump, digging in with his claws. Manfred trumpeted in pain. Sid continued to steer the mammoth down the slide, now with Diego as a passenger.

Roshan whizzed through a nearby tunnel, bouncing lightly on his pelt. He waved his arms and gurgled, enjoying the ride.

A second later the animals flowed into separate ice loops, zipping through them as though trapped in an enormous crazy straw. The loops flung them in different directions before all three swooped back together again.

Sid screamed—he was on a collision course with Manfred and Diego, *swooshing* through another chute.

But their funnels were actually above and below his, so they all *whooshed* past one another. Then the slides twisted around in bewildering spirals. When the animals straightened out, they were all gliding in the same direction in straight chutes right next to one another.

Manfred, Diego, and Sid flowed down the sleek slides on their backs. They pressed their limbs close to their sides to make them move faster, teeming down the straightaway toward Roshan up ahead. Then, right in front of him, Sid noticed a solid wall of ice filling the cave from floor to ceiling. There was no way he could stop. He smashed into the wall at full speed and slammed through it, with Diego right behind him. Manfred managed to catch Roshan just before flying through the wall himself.

When the snow and ice settled, Manfred and Sid

sat perfectly still, dazed from their dizzying ride. A moment later Diego popped out from under a mound of snow.

"*Whoooooaaa!*" he cheered, as excited and frisky as a kitten. "Who's up for round two?" He held up his paw for a highfive. Manfred and Sid glared at Diego. From the expressions on their faces, he could tell they were not in a high-five sort of mood. "Um, ahem." He cleared his throat in an attempt to sound more serious. "Tell the kid to be more careful."

CHAPTER NINE

Underneath the glacier, Diego, Sid, and Manfred investigated the gigantic cavern where they had landed. The walls were covered with paintings of humans and animals in all sorts of situations.

Sid pointed to a group of crudely drawn big cats. "Look," he said. "Tigers!" He followed the trail of tigers, grimacing at a painting that showed a saber-tooth attacking an antelope. "*Yeesh*." Sid groaned.

Roshan waggled his fingers at the tiger paintings, looking frightened.

"It's okay," Sid whispered to the baby. "Look, the tigers are just playing tag with the antelopes." Then the sloth glanced at Diego and smirked at him. "With their *teeth*."

Diego shrugged, picking at his fangs with a sharp claw. "C'mon, Sid," the tiger growled. "Let's play tag. You're it."

Sid laughed nervously and quickly turned to examine the paintings again. "So, um . . . where are the sloths?" he asked. "You never see any sloths in these things."

As he searched, Sid spotted a sketch of a massive animal. "Look, Manny," he called. "A mammoth!"

"*Ooo*," Manfred said flatly. "Somebody pinch me."

Sid peered more closely at the drawing. "Hey, this fat one looks like you," the sloth noted, pointing at a male mammoth. Near the male was a slightly smaller female beside a little calf. "Aw, he's got a family."

That got Manfred's attention. He shuffled closer to the drawing, standing between Diego and Sid. A disturbed expression flickered in Manfred's eyes.

"He's happy," Sid added, tracing the sketch with his finger. "Look, he's playing with his kid. See, Manny? That's your problem, that's what mammoths are supposed to do—"

"Sid," Diego broke in, his voice filled with warning.

"Find a she-mammoth," Sid continued, not noticing Manfred's distress. "Have a little baby mammoth—"

"*Sid,*" Diego repeated, more urgently.

"What?" Sid shot back, annoyed.

"Shut up," the tiger ordered.

Sid opened his arms wide in protest. "But . . ." He glanced at the mammoth and finally noticed the pain in Manfred's eyes. He let his sentence trail off. "Oh."

As Manfred stared at the drawings, the still images began to move in his mind, coming alive. He remembered playing happily in a lush meadow with his wife and his child, romping in the sunshine until a horde of humans ran out of the woods, waving their spears fiercely.

Manfred faced off against the hunters, trying to hold them back with his imposing tusks. Behind him, his family ran to find shelter. Then Manfred heard a deep, terrified scream. He wheeled around and saw that his mate and child were trapped against a rock wall by humans aiming spears at them.

Before Manfred could move, another group of humans dropped heavy rocks from atop the rock wall.

Bellowing in anguish, Manfred saw his family being crushed by the rocks. His cries shook the landscape, echoing off the rocks all around.

Back in the cavern, the mammoth shook his head, clearing the devastating memory from his mind. He breathed heavily, trying to regain control of his runaway emotions.

Sid and Diego stared at Manfred with worried eyes. Then they turned back to the painting, clearing their throats uncomfortably.

Manfred kept staring at the cave drawings. He gazed at the sketch of the father mammoth cradling his young child in his trunk. Slowly, Manfred raised his own trunk toward the illustration.

Before he could reach it, Roshan's tiny hand touched the drawing gently. He was standing on his feet, propped up against the cave wall.

Surprised, Manfred pulled back his trunk. He blinked at the little human boy.

Roshan stroked the picture of the baby mammoth with his fingers, glancing back at the mammoth as though he was connecting the two in his mind. Then Roshan stumbled toward Manfred.

Manfred caught the baby with his trunk. He slowly lifted Roshan off the ground. He curled his trunk, hugging Roshan close, nuzzling his cheek against the baby's head.

Sid sniffled, wiping a glob of snot from his nose with his paw onto Diego. Manfred swooped Roshan onto his back and walked out of the cave without a word. Sid followed. Diego took one last look at the painting of the mammoth family and let out a sad sigh, then sauntered out of the cave after the others.

Deep in the glacial valley, Runar led his hunters across a snowy plain. Their wolves pulled on their leashes, sniffing the ground like hunting dogs. The humans stopped beside a set of footprints to examine them, but then they shook their heads sadly. They weren't tiger tracks.

The wolves sniffed around, digging their noses in the snow, but they seemed confused. Runar tightened his grip on one wolf's leash—he had to admit that the wolves had lost the scent. One of the hunters came over and took the leash from Runar's grip.

With a deep sigh, the chief looked down at his son's broken necklace in his hand. He shook his head, giving up hope.

He had to lead his people through Glacier Pass to their settlement on the other side before the snow made that trip impossible.

With a heavy heart, Runar followed his hunters back toward the rest of the tribe.

Outside the cavern, the animals found themselves on the edge of a wide, flat field of snowy white. Manfred plucked Roshan off his back and held him in his trunk as they rested. At the other end of the expanse, a partially crumbled volcano loomed in the distance.

"Well, would you look at that," Manfred said, sounding amazed. "The tiger actually did it. There's Half-Peak. Next stop, Glacier Pass." The mammoth glanced at the tiger, nodding respectfully. "How did I ever doubt you?"

Sid scampered over to Roshan. "Did you hear that? You're almost home!"

Manfred planted the baby back up on his broad shoulders. Then the mammoth and the tiger hurried away across the field of snow. Roshan waved back at Sid.

Sid caught up to them, then stopped to peer down at his hind paws. "My feet are sweating," he muttered to himself, confused.

Diego groaned. "Do we have to get a news flash every time your body does something?"

Sid hopped closer to them, his feet steaming. "Seriously," he called, "my feet are really hot." Behind him, his pawprints melted and bubbled in the snow.

A low, deep rumble shook the field, echoing off the surrounding mountains. Diego and Manfred stopped in their tracks, looking around.

"Tell me that was your stomach," Manfred said uneasily.

"*Shh!*" Diego hissed, listening with his ears perked up. The sudden silence in the field was unnerving.

"I'm sure it was just thunder," Sid said.

Another terrifying rumble shook the ground. The animals tottered on their feet.

"From under . . . ground," Sid added with a gulp.

With a deafening explosion, a wad of bright orange lava blasted out of the earth. The ball of molten rock sizzled through the air, a stream of smoke trailing out behind it.

All around, lava globs burst out of the ground with the sound of cannon fire, whizzing into the sky.

"Run!" the animals screamed.

CHAPTER TEN

Pieces of the field began to disappear in clouds of white steam, leaving nothing but narrow bridges of ice for Manfred, Sid, and Diego to stand on. Underneath them, glowing magma seeped out of fissures in the earth, forming sizzling rivers of lava all around.

The path in front of Sid was melting with terrifying speed. The sloth tried to run, but the surface was too slippery. "C'mon!" he called to the mammoth. "Keep up with me!"

"I would if you were moving!" Manfred hollered.

Sid slipped and fell down on his face. With a bone-jarring jolt, the section of the bridge between Diego and Manfred suddenly cracked and tumbled away. Diego was stuck on a thin piece of ice. Sid and Manfred stared at him from their bridge across the ravine.

The tiger looked down at the bubbling lava beneath him. Then he leaped, soaring over the gap. He landed safely on the bridge that held Manfred and Sid.

"Wow," Sid said. "I wish I could jump like that."

Manfred peered around Sid, who was blocking his exit off the bridge. "Wish granted," the mammoth muttered. With a swift kick, Manfred punted the sloth into the air.

Sid screamed in terror as he soared off the ice. He landed safely far from the lava, facefirst in the snow.

With Sid out of his way, Manfred cautiously made his way across the crumbling bridge. Now Diego was stuck behind the mammoth with no room to pass. "C'mon!" the tiger growled. "Move faster!"

"Have you noticed the river of lava?" Manfred pointed out.

With an ear-splitting crack, a slim section of ice broke away right in front of Manfred. He looked down through the new hole and got a very clear view of the molten death waiting below.

Taking a deep breath, Manfred leaped across the

crack. He landed heavily on the edge of the ice on the other side, then hurried to safe ground near Sid.

As Diego tried to make the same jump, though, the crack suddenly gaped wider as the last piece of bridge melted into the lava.

The tiger caught the icy ledge on the far side with his claws—barely hanging on.

"*Diego!*" Sid shrieked.

Manfred turned around to look. When he saw the tiger dangling over the edge, he shoved Roshan into Sid's arms. "Hold Pinky," the mammoth said. Then he strode to the frozen cliff to help Diego.

The ledge was melting, too—it slumped at an odd angle as it teetered over the fiery pit. Diego scrambled to keep hold.

Too nervous to watch anymore, Sid covered his eyes with one paw, Roshan's with his other.

Manfred eased himself closer to the edge as Diego slipped a little more, his claws slicing through the ice. Then the tiger's claws pulled completely free from the ledge and he started to fall.

Whipping out his trunk, Manfred snagged its tip around the tiger's leg. The mammoth backed up, yanking Diego over his head and onto the cliff.

With a sickening lurch, the remaining bit of the bridge Manfred was on broke into tiny pieces. The mammoth tumbled down into the pit with the last of the ice.

"Manny!" Sid cried. For a long moment, Sid and Diego stared in horror at the spot where their friend had disappeared. Then an enormous explosion erupted out of the fiery abyss.

Sid and Diego ducked as rocks, chunks of ice, and solid strips of lava blasted up from the depths of the pit. Along with the rocketing debris, Manfred soared up, propelled by the devastating explosion. The mammoth crashed on the ledge with a heavy thud that dented the ground.

Sid and Roshan hurried to Manfred's side. Roshan crawled on top of Manfred, tenderly stroking his furry head.

"Manny?" Sid whispered, nudging the mammoth to see if he was still alive. "Manny, you okay?" Then the sloth pushed Manfred's body, shaking him gently. "C'mon, say something," Sid demanded. "Anything!"

For a long moment, the huge body of the mammoth lay silent where it had fallen.

"You're standing on my trunk," Manfred said weakly.

"*Yay!*" Sid cheered, raising his scrawny arms over his head. "You're okay!"

Diego got up and walked over to Manfred. "Why did you do that?" he asked softly. "You could've died trying to save me."

"That's what you do in a herd," Manfred replied. "You look out for each other."

"Well. . ." Diego mumbled, lowering his head. "Thanks."

Manfred started walking toward Half-Peak, and after a second Diego followed.

"We're the weirdest herd I've ever seen," Sid put in as he trailed after the mammoth and the tiger.

———————

By the time darkness fell that evening, the travelers had hiked most of the way up the slope to Half-Peak. A cold wind whipped over the glaciers all around them. In the dark, the climb was so difficult that even Manfred and Diego struggled to put one paw in front of the other.

Manfred slowed down and nodded his big head toward a rocky formation with curved walls. "Guys, we've gotta get the baby out of the wind," he said.

They all took shelter behind the stone shield. As soon as they were protected from the wind, its constant howl dropped to a faint whisper.

"How much farther?" Manfred asked Diego.

Diego rested his eyes wearily. "Three miles."

Manfred nodded. He stepped onto a fat dead log so he could peer over the top of the rock shelter. A vast glacial landscape was spread out all around them. Its frozen ridges resembled the surface of the moon. As Manfred looked around, his gaze settled on the looming top of Half-Peak. It was only a short journey away.

Ducking back into the shelter, Manfred sat down with an exhausted sigh. "We'll get there in the morning," he decided. "I'm beat."

Diego watched as Sid picked up a small rock and began drawing on the shelter's wall. "What are you doing?" the tiger asked.

"Putting sloths on the map," Sid replied. He sketched out a round body, giving it stick arms and legs and a head with a snout.

"Make it more realistic," Manfred suggested. "Draw him lying down."

"And make him rounder," Diego said.

Manfred snatched the rock away from Sid with his trunk. On the wall, the mammoth drew a chubby, pear-shaped sloth relaxing.

"And stupider," Diego added.

"Ha, ha, ha," Sid replied flatly. He grabbed the rock away from Manfred and scratched it roughly against the wall, trying to rub out the mammoth's drawing.

A spark shot from the scraping rock. It fell into a pile of dried leaves, which curled up as they started to burn. The animals all stared at the tiny fire, stunned.

"*Ooo!*" Sid gasped, gazing at the flames. "I'm a

genius!" He hurried over to the dead log and broke off a few branches. Then he fed them to the fire, stoking it up hot.

A short while later, everybody stretched out around a blazing bonfire, enjoying its warm glow. Roshan, rosy-cheeked from the firelight, held out his little hands toward the flames, getting them nice and toasty. Sid lounged beside the baby, smiling with pride as he basked in the heat. "From now on, just call me 'Sid, Lord of the Flame,'" he told the others.

"Hey, Lord of the Flame," Manfred said, arching a woolly eyebrow. "Your tail's on fire."

Sid hopped to his feet and let out a yelp. When he saw the flames on his tail, he panicked and immediately tripped over a rock, falling onto his face.

Diego snuffed out the little fire with his paw.

"*Ahhh . . .*" Sid moaned in relief. He turned to smile gratefully at the tiger. "Thank you. From now on I'm gonna call you 'Diego—'"

"Lord of touch me and you're dead," Diego broke in.

Sid gasped, stepping away from the tiger nervously. Then Diego laughed and threw his paw around Sid's shoulders. He gave the sloth a rough noogie on his skull. "I'm just kidding, you little knucklehead."

"Hey, lovebirds," Manfred called. His voice sounded hushed and excited as he gestured with his trunk toward Roshan. "Look at this. . ."

Diego and Sid peered at the baby. Roshan was standing. He wobbled but stayed upright without grabbing on to anything.

"I don't believe it," Sid breathed.

Lifting his feet, Roshan took his first steps, toddling slowly. He grinned at the animals. They stared back at him, smiling, feeling stunned and proud.

"Come here, you little biped," Sid cajoled Roshan. "Come here, you little wormy worm, come to Uncle Sid."

Roshan waddled toward Sid for a second, then stumbled in Diego's direction.

Diego shooed the baby away with his paw. "No, no," he said. "Go to Sid."

Roshan toddled closer to Diego. He stumbled, falling onto the tiger's legs. Roshan grabbed one leg and held on, hugging it tight.

Raising his paw, Diego helped Roshan stand again. "Uh . . . okay," the tiger mumbled, sounding uncomfortable. "Good job." Diego nudged Roshan with his muzzle, pushing him away. "Keep practicing."

Roshan faced Sid, grinning.

Sid beamed back at the baby. "Aw," he said with a sigh, "our little guy's growing up."

The baby took one more step and then plopped backward onto his butt. He immediately yawned and rubbed his eyes sleepily.

"All right," Manfred said. He scooped Roshan up with his trunk. "C'mon," he murmured. "Sleep time, lumpy."

Sid reclined on the ground near Diego. "Look at that big pushover," the sloth said, watching the mammoth cuddle the baby.

Manfred gently rocked Roshan in the curve of his trunk, nuzzling him fondly.

"You know, Diego," Sid whispered, "I never had a friend who would risk his life for me."

"Yeah, Manny's a good guy," Diego said.

Sid turned his head until he was looking right into the tiger's golden eyes.

"Yeah," the sloth said firmly. "He is." Then Sid yawned and turned onto his side. "Well, good night."

As Sid started snoring, Diego stepped away from the campfire. He stared up at the blanket of stars glittering in the inky sky, his conflicting emotions flickering on his face.

A light dusting of snow trickled down through the firelight.

CHAPTER ELEVEN

In the morning, the sky was slate gray as the animals continued their trek up to Half-Peak. The bleak, chill air pressed down on the travelers like a heavy blanket, making the landscape seem eerily quiet and still.

As they marched through a trail between two tall ridges of rock, Diego kept peering around nervously. "Maybe we shouldn't do this," the tiger said.

"Why not?" Sid asked.

"Because if we save him, he'll grow up to be a hunter," Diego replied crankily. "And who do you think he'll hunt? *Us.*"

Sid shrugged. "Maybe because we save him, he won't hunt us."

"Oh, yeah," Diego replied sarcastically. "And maybe he'll grow fur and a long, skinny neck and call you Mama."

Roshan giggled.

Manfred stared at Diego. "What's your problem?"

"Nothing," Diego replied, his fur bristling in irritation. "I'm freezing my tail off." He loped ahead, and the others followed.

The animals walked out of the pass and entered a small, snowy clearing. They stopped, staring up at the stunning view of Half-Peak above them. The partially collapsed volcanic cone loomed with haunting, craggy beauty, making the mammals feel very small in comparison.

The tiger let the sloth and the mammoth pass him. Glancing around, Diego glimpsed a flash of saber fur vanishing behind a rock on the next hill.

A look of bewildered misery clouded the tiger's golden eyes. He stared straight ahead, watching as Manfred and Sid wandered directly toward the trap he had led them to.

"Hey, Diego," Manfred called, glancing behind him. "You frozen back there?"

Struggling painfully with himself to make the

right decision, Diego grimaced and narrowed his eyes, his breath thickening in his throat. The tiger stared at his companions as they walked ever closer to the point of no return. Against the snow, with the massive volcano behind them, Manfred, Sid, and Roshan looked so vulnerable that Diego's heart lurched.

"Get down!" the tiger roared.

Manfred wheeled around to face him. "What?"

"*Shh!*" Diego hissed. "Get down and follow me!" He quickly herded his companions behind a protective curved lip of ice, peering around anxiously.

"What's going on?" Sid whispered.

The tiger took a deep breath. "At the bottom of Half-Peak there's an ambush waiting for you."

"*What?*" Sid gasped.

"What do you mean, *ambush*?" Manfred demanded. He paused, his hackles rising as he realized what had happened. "You set us up."

Diego lowered his head. "It was my job," he explained. "I was supposed to get the baby, but then—"

"You brought us home for dinner," Manfred finished angrily.

"That's it!" Sid yelled, pointing a claw at the tiger. "You're out of the herd!"

"I'm sorry," Diego whispered, closing his eyes.

"No, you're not," Manfred said. He lunged forward, pinning Diego against the wall of ice between his tusks. "Not yet."

"Listen," Diego said. "I can help you—"

Manfred ignored the tiger. "Stay close, Sid," he told the sloth. "We can fight our way out."

"You can't," Diego said rapidly. "The pack's too strong. You have to trust me."

Manfred shifted a tusk so that its razor-sharp point was pressed against Diego's throat like a knife. "*Trust* you?" Manfred growled. "Why in the world would we trust you?"

Diego stared deeply into the mammoth's huge eyes. "Because I'm your only chance," he replied.

———————

Up at the pinnacle of Half-Peak, the pack of saber-toothed tigers were crouched behind twisted lava towers, twitching their tails in anticipation. As they spotted an approaching animal, they tensed, ready to pounce.

Diego trotted over to them, his golden eyes glowing in the morning light. "Hello, ladies," he greeted the other tigers.

"Hey, look who decided to show up," Oscar called obnoxiously.

Diego glared at Oscar silently as Soto slunk out of the shadows.

"Diego," Soto growled. "I was beginning to worry about you."

"No need to worry," Diego replied. "In about two minutes you'll be satisfying your taste for revenge."

"Is it alive?" Soto demanded.

Diego nodded. "And kicking."

Soto licked his lips. "Very nice," he murmured.

In the clearing below the tigers, Sid waddled into the open. The sloth carried Roshan in a fur blanket, with the baby tucked deeply in its warm folds. Sid glanced around warily as he marched across the snow.

Zeke peered around the lava formation he was hiding behind. "I see the sloth!" he whimpered, bristling with insane excitement. "And he's got the baby!"

Soto growled at him. "Don't give away your positions until you see the mammoth!" he ordered sternly. "He's the one we have to surprise."

As Zeke watched the sloth's progress across the clearing, he began to hyperventilate, desperately eager to pounce.

Diego put his mouth up to the crazy tiger's ear. "You wanna maul something," he whispered, "don't you, Zeke?"

Zeke stuffed his own paw into his mouth, stifling

his impatient whimpering. "Yeah, yeah, I wanna maul." He groaned.

Diego glanced over at the other tigers—they weren't paying attention, all completely focused on Sid. He waited a moment for the sloth to reach the halfway point across the clearing. Then he leaned down to Zeke's ear again. "Then what are you waiting for? *Now*, Zeke," he whispered urgently. "Get him!"

Zeke bolted out from behind the lava tower, rushing toward Sid.

The other tigers bounded out from their hiding places, too.

"No!" Soto howled in fury. "I said, wait for the mammoth!"

The tigers stopped and turned back, confused. But it was too late—their positions had already been revealed, losing the advantage of surprise.

"Forget it!" Soto roared. "Get the baby!"

Sid let out a shriek as the pack of tigers galloped toward him. He jumped above the layer of snow that had been covering his feet. He was wearing wooden skis!

Instantly, Sid launched himself down a steep slope, zipping across the snow. He whizzed on the skis, keeping just ahead of the tigers chasing behind him.

With a bump, Sid zoomed up a small hill that acted like a ramp. He soared into the air, clutching

Roshan to his chest. After a second, Sid landed again with a jarring thump and almost lost his balance. But he managed to regain control and kept sliding ahead of the tigers.

Then he bashed into a hidden rock, losing one ski. Sid continued to zip forward, performing amazing snowboarding moves on his single ski.

When he had gained some distance, Sid relaxed a little. He turned his head and made a goofy face at the tigers while performing a fancy ski move, zipping along on one paw. "Nah-nah!" the sloth taunted the tigers chasing him. "Nah—"

Then Sid lost his balance again. He stumbled, tumbling into the air and losing his last ski. The fur-wrapped baby flew out of Sid's arms and skidded over the ice.

Roaring, Soto rushed over and snatched the fur bundle up in his mouth. The blanket fell open and lumps of crumbling snow and ice tumbled out of it. Instead of Roshan, Soto found a snow baby—complete with little eyes, a nose, and a smile.

Soto smashed the snow baby apart, howling with rage.

Sid landed near a formation of crumbling, bare rock. He hopped to his feet and turned to face the tigers. "Sorry, fellas!" he called to them, waving cheerfully. "He caught a little cold!"

"Get him!" Soto screamed.

Oscar and Lenny bolted toward Sid, snarling.

Sid hurried around the pile of rocks.

When Oscar and Lenny pounced around the corner, they stopped short, gazing up at the huge mammoth waiting for them.

Manfred held a large spike of lava in his tusks. He brandished it like a baseball bat. *"Surprise!"*

He swung the spike, whacking both tigers at once. The spike shattered as the tigers were bashed off a ledge.

On the other side of the boulder stack, Sid waddled off the path, trying to escape along a rocky trail.

Zeke spotted the sloth and smiled evilly. The tiger slunk after the sloth, drooling.

Meanwhile, Diego rushed over to Manfred and they both peered at the unconscious bodies of Oscar and Lenny in the snow below them. "Okay, follow me," Diego told the mammoth. "We'll get Sid and get out of here while we can."

Then Soto slunk around the corner of the boulder pile, his eyes blazing furiously.

"C'mon, Diego," Soto hissed. "Let's bring this mammoth down."

Sid strode farther away, following a rough path between huge boulders. The sloth stopped beside another pile of volcanic stones. He reached into a hollow depression in one of the rocks and pulled Roshan out of his hiding spot.

Behind him, Zeke's wild eyes lit up with delight when he saw the baby. He hunkered down, ready to pounce.

Sid stiffened, sensing the tiger's presence. He ducked, screaming, and Zeke leaped over his head.

The tiger missed Sid completely. He soared head-first into the hollow where Roshan had been hiding. Zeke tried to yank his head free, but it was stuck tight in the narrow space.

With a cheer, Sid began to hop up and down on Zeke's rump, wedging him farther into the hollow. "Survival of the fittest?" Sid exclaimed. "I don't think so!"

He and Roshan gave each other a high five.

Diego snarled as he faced off against Soto, standing between the leader of the tigers and Manfred. As Soto padded closer, Diego backed up slowly.

A look of confusion flickered on Soto's furious face. "What are you *doing?*" he growled at Diego.

Stopping short, Diego glared at Soto. "Leave the mammoth alone," he hissed.

Behind Manfred, Lenny and Oscar woke up from their fall and climbed back over the ledge.

When Soto saw that the two members of his pack were conscious, he smiled, then focused his attention back on Diego. "Fine," Soto seethed. "I'll take you down first."

With a terrifying roar, Soto lashed out at Diego.

Diego lunged at the leader of the tiger pack. They both growled and snarled as they battled intensely, rearing up on their hind legs. The tigers locked their claws around each other's shoulders, struggling for the upper hand in the vicious fight.

While Diego was busy battling Soto, Manfred trumpeted anxiously as Lenny and Oscar swiped at him with their sharp claws, backing him up against the rock wall.

Soto roared again. With a vicious whack of his paw, he bashed Diego backward. Shaking off the painful blow, Diego charged, but Soto smacked him again, sending him reeling into the snow. Diego collapsed on his side and lay still on the ground.

With a smile, Soto turned back toward the mammoth. He paced closer to Manfred, padding between

98

Lenny and Oscar, thrilled at the fear on the mammoth's face.

Behind him, Diego raised his head. He struggled to climb back to his paws.

Soto, Lenny, and Oscar slowly advanced on Manfred.

Manfred glanced around. There was no way to escape.

Soto grinned, his eyes blazing with menace. He lowered his head, and pounced at Manfred, ready to finish him off.

Leaping in front of the mammoth, Diego intercepted Soto's attack. One of Soto's razor-sharp sabers sliced into Diego's gut. Diego roared in pain as he collapsed at Manfred's feet.

"You asked for it!" Soto screeched. He reached back with a gleaming claw to finish Diego off.

Nearby, Roshan cried out when he saw that Diego was hurt.

Soto paused, distracted by the baby's cry. He peered around until he spotted Sid not far away, holding Roshan in his arms.

Manfred lashed his trunk out violently at Soto, whipping him off Diego.

Howling, Soto shot up in the air and whacked into another section of the rocky wall. He landed on his back, dazed by the blow.

A frozen overhang curled above his head, its sharp icicles swinging like wind chimes. The icicles broke off and plummeted down, whizzing toward the leader of the saber-toothed tigers.

Manfred and Sid turned away. Sid covered Roshan's eyes, shielding them from the gruesome sight.

CHAPTER TWELVE

Manfred peered around at the remaining tigers in the area. Oscar, Zeke, and Lenny stared in horror at their fallen leader. All their spirit had drained out of them. When Manfred growled at them, the deflated tigers quickly loped away, vanishing down the trail to the valley below.

Diego moaned weakly. He lay on his side, breathing heavily.

"Diego!" Manfred cried. He, Sid, and Roshan hurried to the tiger and hovered over him worriedly.

"We were some team, huh?" Diego asked softly.

"C'mon, we're *still* a team," Manfred replied.

Diego feebly raised his head. "I'm sorry I set you up," he whispered, struggling to breathe.

"Ah, you know me," Sid said gently. "I'm too lazy to hold a grudge."

The tiger smiled and lowered his head to the snow again. Roshan reached out to stroke Diego's soft chin. "Hey, knock it off, squirt. I'll be okay. But you have to take care of Manfred and Sid now. Especially Sid."

"Come on, you can lick this," Sid encouraged Diego. "Look, I'll carry you. What do you say?"

"Listen," Diego went on. "You have to leave me here. If those humans get through the pass you'll never catch them. You'll have to return the little guy without me."

"We will," Manfred promised. Then the mammoth blinked away a tear. "You didn't have to do that," he told the tiger, his voice heavy with sorrow.

Diego held Manfred's gaze meaningfully. "That's what you do in a herd," he whispered. Manfred smiled and nodded at the tiger's heartfelt words.

A tear trickled down Sid's face, freezing on his cheek. He and Manfred stared down at the wounded tiger, their shoulders limp with sadness. Roshan kept patting Diego's head, sobbing quietly, until Manfred picked him up and hugged him.

The next morning, as dawn brightened the sky, Sid and Manfred trudged wearily up a hill through deep snow. Atop the mammoth's back, Roshan snuggled in his dense fur, tucked in deeply to stay warm.

After a short journey, Manfred and Sid reached Glacier Pass. The humans, led by Runar, were heading through the narrow route open between two huge blocks of ice. The chief, certain he would never see his son again, stopped for a moment to place Roshan's necklace on a mound of snow. When he stood up, Manfred and Sid were standing before him.

Unsure of their intentions, Runar quickly raised his spear in defense. Manfred reached out with his trunk and grabbed it, then tossed the spear to the ground. The other humans charged toward the mammoth, ready to attack. But then Roshan popped out of Manfred's fur and gurgled.

Runar's eyes grew wide and he signaled for his men to fall back. Manfred gently handed Roshan to his father. As soon as his son was in his arms, Runar hugged him tightly, pressing his cheek against the top of the baby's head.

Sid and Manfred turned to go, their mission complete. As they moved away, Roshan squirmed in his father's arms. Runar let the baby slide to the ground. Roshan toddled as fast as he could after Manfred and Sid, squealing for them to stop.

The mammoth and the sloth turned around as Roshan tottered closer. Manfred reached out with his trunk and gently scooped up the baby, cuddling him.

Sid sniffled loudly. "Don't forget about us, okay?"

"We won't forget about you," Manfred promised, handing him back to his father. Manfred met Runar's gaze and Runar nodded, thanking the mammoth in silence. He plucked Roshan's necklace out of the snow and gratefully draped it over one of Manfred's tusks.

Runar carried Roshan back to the group and the entire tribe entered Glacier Pass. "Good-bye," Sid called as he waved, tears rolling down his face. "Good-bye." He watched as the humans grew smaller and smaller in the distance. Then he noticed Roshan had covered his eyes and was playing peekaboo. Sid played along, trying to smile. "That's right! Where's the baby?"

"Come on, Sid," Manfred said. "Let's head south." He turned away as the humans vanished over the hill—and froze in his tracks. Diego was limping toward them.

"Good-bye," Sid said one final time.

"Save your breath, Sid. You know humans can't talk."

The sloth whirled around when he heard that familiar voice, his face lighting up with joy. "Diego! You're okay!"

"Nine lives, baby."

Sid ran to him, tackled him playfully, then planted a big kiss right on his nose.

Manfred wandered over. "Welcome back, partner. Want a lift?"

"No, thanks. I've got to save whatever dignity I've got left."

"You're hanging out with us now," Sid announced. "You left dignity behind a long time ago. I'll take that lift, though."

"Climb aboard."

"*Woo-hoo!*" Sid crowed. "Pick me up, buddy!"

Grabbing Sid with his trunk, Manfred placed the sloth on top of his broad, hairy back.

"*Yee-ha!*" Sid cheered as he took a seat on the mammoth. "Mush!"

Turning his head, Manfred glared at the sloth.

"Or . . . not mush," Sid said weakly. "Either way. This is gonna be the best migration ever, I'm telling you. I'll show you all my favorite watering holes. You know, I turn brown when all the fungus in my fur dries out."

"Sounds very attractive," Diego commented, loping slowly alongside.

Together they headed across a wide field of snow. In the distance, a range of magnificent mountain peaks loomed, their ice caps glistening in the brilliant sunshine.

E P I L O G U E

On the horizon, a craggy shape bobbed in the ocean, close to shore. A little squirrel-like critter was frozen inside. It was the scrat, still clutching his acorn, encased in his own tiny iceberg.

The mini-iceberg washed ashore and the scrat stared out at the surf, unable to move. The ice around the acorn melted and it tumbled into the sand. A wave immediately caught it and washed it out to sea. The scrat blinked in horror at his disappearing acorn, then let out a miserable scream and broke free of the ice. Running blindly, he smacked right into a coconut tree. A coconut dropped into the sand beside him and he jumped for joy. He grabbed the coconut and raced off with it down the beach.

The scrat raised the coconut over his head, then jammed it down into the sand with all his might, trying to store it. With a frighteningly loud groan, a zigzagging crack appeared in the sand under the coconut. The scrat watched with wide, frightened eyes as the crack lengthened, unzipping across the beach. The fissure snaked into the jungle, swished through trees, seared rocks in half, and scurried up to the summit of a dormant volcano.

Ka-boom! Fire and smoke belched out of the erupting mountain. Here we go again.